The Courtship of the Clauses

C.C. Marley

DEDICATION

To I &K, my muses, and the embodiment of magic and merriment.

And to the memory of Charles Dickens, whose simple Christmas tale revitalized the

spirit of a weary world.

It is easy to forget that Santa and Mrs. Claus were not always the way we know them now. They were not always the gentle and genteel symbols of our world's most beloved holiday.

They were not born old. They were not born married. Or even particularly notable. This is how it all came to pass...

***

It was a year whose number no one can quite remember or confirm, as it was so very long ago. The exact time or location where our story begins is unimportant. The destiny of the Clauses would have transpired the same no matter time or place. For once in a while, two people are born with a purpose so important, so certain to be a force for good in a sometimes not very good world, that even space and time cede their powers to help fulfill that destiny.

***

Nicholas was born on a cold day in a cold village to cold people, who had not wanted him. But Nicholas? He was as warm as the very sun itself. As he grew, his mother and father sought to diminish his warmth, and used everything within their powers to convey their own anger and bitterness, about everything and nothing, onto their child. It was to no avail, however, as their efforts served only to galvanize Nicholas' longing to be good and decent and kind. His heart was as full and pure as his parents' hearts were empty and decayed. Though his family was desperately poor, he grew ever more grateful and generous day by day.

In a village nearby, a beautiful baby girl had been born on the same day, at the same time, as Nicholas, to the wealthiest family in the entire realm, whose vast fortune afforded them every luxury. Hers was a childhood of privilege and indulgence; she was beloved by all and denied nothing. Still, despite the tendency for such unfailing adoration to damage a child's nature, making them spoiled and petulant and hardening their heart to the suffering in the world, this was never true for Lark, as she was called, in honor of the songbirds that heralded her birth.

It may seem quite unlikely that the paths of these two children, one raised in squalor, one in splendor, would ever cross. But cross they did, because the world needed for it to happen. And when they did, extraordinary things followed.

***

It was one of those bitterly cold days that leave your warm breath hanging visibly in the air and your body chilled to the bone. That morning, Nicholas left his home dressed in the warmest clothes he had, which were threadbare and entirely unsuited to the harsh conditions. He was a sturdy boy, strong but gentle, with dark hair and lashes, and twinkling eyes of the deepest blue.

Meanwhile, Lark was attended by her servants and maids who bundled her in the finest clothing and furs so she could go on her daily walk around the grounds. She never minded the cold, insisting on exploring outdoors regardless of the weather. Her auburn curls were tucked neatly under her fur trimmed hat, and her plump cheeks became immediately ruddy when she stepped outside into the cold air.

On this particular day, she happened to find herself lost in the vast forest surrounding her family's estate. Although she had an adventurous spirit, Lark was not in the habit of straying too far from the safety of home. This day, however, she was distracted by a small fox whose path she followed deep into the forest. He was black as soot, which was as strange a thing as Lark had ever seen. By the time she realized just how far she had strayed, she found herself in a clearing, surrounded by towering trees and a growing sense of dread. She was not a fearful child, but there was something foreboding about the silence that now enveloped her, and the darkness from the trees blotting out the bright winter sun. After considering the situation, Lark found that all she was prepared to do was sit on the forest floor, and wait, and worry. She was not accustomed to being particularly self-reliant, as she had simply never had to be.

Nicholas' journey that morning took him through the same forest, as he prepared to go into the village center to ask if any of the shopkeepers or tradesmen needed help that day. It was his daily ritual, since his parents expected him to earn his own keep, providing for their son barely the essentials necessary to survive. This particular day, he had decided to take the long way through the forest. Nicholas knew the forest well, as he often spent time there when his mother and father sent him out of the house for the simple reason that they wished him gone. Gentle spirit that he was, the forest animals quickly learned to trust him, and would gather to keep him company when he visited.

Now it happens that this particular day, he was greeted by a black fox whom he had never seen before in these woods. The fox did not seem to share the other animals' comfort with Nicholas, and darted away when the two encountered one another. Nicholas was disappointed, as he always enjoyed befriending new creatures, but continued happily along his way, in the same direction as the fox.

A little further into the forest, he began to hear a faint noise that sounded like crying. He stood still a moment, listening, until he could determine where the sound was coming from. Then he quickly but carefully pursued it, always eager to help someone in distress.

Eventually, he came to a clearing and was startled to see a girl there, sitting on the forest floor, crying. He had never encountered another living soul except for the animals on his journeys through these woods, but he did not linger in that thought. He cleared his throat quietly, so that his sudden appearance didn't frighten her, and she immediately lifted her hooded head, which had been buried in her arms, her knees drawn tightly to her.

She gasped when she saw Nicholas, but something about his presence immediately calmed her.

"Hello," Nicholas said in a quiet voice, with a warm smile, as he extended his hand to her.

"Hello," Lark replied weakly, wiping away a remaining tear with her mittened hand before taking his.

As he helped her to her feet he said, "My name is Nicholas. I heard you crying, are you hurt?" his eyes were filled with worry and she quickly answered "No, no, nothing like that. I'm just terribly lost." He noticed her large green eyes were again beginning to well up with tears so he said gently, "Oh please don't be afraid. I can help you!"

She smiled a small smile and asked, "But how? I don't have any idea how I got here, so I don't know how you could help."

"I'm not sure." Nicholas said, "but I know I can figure something out! Why don't you start by telling me your name, and we'll go from there?" he smiled at her.

"Oh yes, I'm very sorry, I seem to have forgotten my manners. Lark. My name is Lark. I live at Helmsgard Manor, and I very much need to get back before everyone becomes worried."

Nicholas grinned broadly, "Helmsgard Manor? Why, that's the most beautiful place in the world!"

Lark laughed modestly at this, and asked, "So you know of it?"

"Know of it?" Nicholas said incredulously, "why, of course! Everyone knows about Helmsgard Manor! They say it was built a thousand years ago by a sorcerer to protect him from dragons and..."

Lark laughed heartily at this, saying, "Oh goodness, dragons?" Then, seeing Nicholas start to look sheepish at his words, quickly added, "But it's true the place is magical! Well, at least it is to me." Now it was her turn to look sheepish as she smiled at her new friend.

"Magical?" Nicholas asked.

"Well, in a way," Lark said thoughtfully. "You see, ever since I could remember, the most wonderful things have happened in my home. Things that can't possibly be explained except by magic. Sometimes it was a candle lighting in the middle of the night by itself or a book I left closed being open when I returned to my room a short time later. Small things, but wonderfully strange, wouldn't you agree?"

Nicholas nodded eagerly, "Oh, yes, I would! I have always believed in magic and I even..." here he trailed off and looked down at the ground.

"You what?" asked Lark, genuinely curious.

"Well," he said quietly, "it's just that...I've always believed I have magic! At least... a little... " again his voice trailed off, unsure of his new friend's response, and frankly surprised at himself for being so open with a stranger. Yet there was something about her that made him almost certain she would never laugh at him or deride him, no matter what he shared.

"Oh, how exciting!" came her response, leaving Nicholas' spirit lifted and his confidence bolstered.

"Yes, isn't it? Of course, it's little things," he said with a smile, "like you said, just something here or there that I can't seem to explain except that somehow I made those things happen."

"Tell me about one of those things, won't you, please?" Lark replied eagerly, her face now aglow with excitement.

An unbridled enthusiasm now overcame Nicholas. What was it about this girl, with her tear-stained face and trusting green eyes that made him feel so warm and comfortable and utterly happy? He didn't know, but he was so delighted to have a seemingly kindred spirit to talk to that he just kept right on talking.

"Well," he began, "there was this one time I was in the village, visiting with Mr. Hallthorp at his wood shop. He seemed upset so I asked him what was wrong. He nodded towards his son, Mathias, who was sitting in the corner, and who looked very sad. I walked over to Mathias and asked what was wrong. He told me he had dropped his favorite toy, a carved wooden horse his father had made for him, into the nearby lake, and could not retrieve it. He was so unhappy, and I felt so helpless. All I could think of to do was close my eyes and wish with all my might that somehow he could be happy again.

The next morning, as I was passing near Mr. Hallthorp's shop, I saw a crowd gathered there and walked over to see what was happening. And there was Mathias, holding a beautifully carved wooden horse and talking excitedly about how it had just somehow appeared on his doorstep that very morning! The villagers who were gathered were disbelieving, saying he must be mistaken, but I knew immediately it was... me. I had made that toy appear! Of course, I had ... have... no idea how, but that wasn't the only time it's happened, there was this one time... "

Realizing he was now talking quite loudly, he paused mid-sentence and said, more quietly, "Well, anyway, that's kind of how it happens. Things just somehow ... appear if I know they are needed. But it only seems to happen with other children; maybe because I know what it's like to need things..." his voice grew faint as he looked at his bare hands, now ashen from the cold.

"Oh, you poor dear!" Lark said, momentarily forgetting his magical tale and focusing entirely on his suffering. Like Nicholas, she was a caring soul, and the pain of others affected her deeply. Removing her own red mittens, she took his hands and placed the mittens on them, rubbing each hand briskly to warm them as she did.

"Oh no, you musn't!" Nicholas cried, but Lark cut him off with a wave of her now-bare hand and a "Hush!"

"My hands are plenty warm now, and yours are like ice. Silly boy, you must have forgotten your mittens this morning!" she said.

"I haven't any mittens." came Nicholas' reply. It was not said with so much as an ounce of self-pity or embarrassment, just as a simple and true declaration.

"Oh," Lark said, "I'm sorry, I didn't realize... " she looked away, seeming to feel the embarrassment that he didn't show. She realized suddenly she had never known anyone who didn't have mittens of their own, and felt ashamed for assuming that everyone must live in the same splendor as she did at Helmsgard Manor. What else did he lack? Did other children suffer from want of basic necessities too? It was a sobering and sad thought, but she didn't want Nicholas to see the effect the realization had had on her, so she responded cheerily with an, "Oh well! You must keep those mittens, then, and I won't hear a word about it!" She smiled at him, and he returned the smile, warmed by it even more than by the mittens which felt so soft and comforting on his chilled, chapped hands.

"Well... okay. But now we must get you home before YOUR hands turn to ice!" he said.

"Yes, but how?" Lark asked.

"Well, I know these woods pretty well, and I know which ways DON'T lead to Helmsgard Manor, so I guess we just take the one that MIGHT!" Nicholas replied confidently. His self-assured manner comforted Lark, and she silently vowed to follow this boy wherever he might go.

The two walked for some time, chatting easily as if they had been friends for an eternity. Eventually, they came to an area Lark recognized and she cried out, "Oh, Nicholas, you were right! This is the way home; you're wonderful!" and without thinking, she flung her arms around him and hugged him with all her strength.

Nicholas had never felt such warmth in his young life, and he closed his eyes and let it wash over him all the way to his toes.

Realizing her passionate outburst might have been unwelcome, Lark pulled herself away from him and began apologizing, but Nicholas would have none of it.

"My goodness, you are strong!" he said, to defuse what he could now see was her embarrassment.

"And I am at your service for as long as you may need." He punctuated this statement with an awkward bow and Lark laughed as he had hoped she would.

"Well, I guess you can find your way back from here." Nicholas said slowly, not wanting his time with this new friend to come to an end.

"Yes, I can!" she replied, adding, "but I am certainly not going a single step without you. You may have saved my life, for all we know, and I need to thank you properly, so you will be our guest for the day!" Her smiling insistence was irresistible, and any objection Nicholas may have been able to create melted away when she smiled at him. He knew his parents would be terribly upset if he didn't bring home any money for them that day, but right now, it seemed completely unimportant. The only thing that mattered to young Nicholas at that moment, was basking in Lark's warmth and approval.

A short while later, the two friends, hand in hand, were coming to the edge of the forest and approaching the path to Helmsgard Manor. Quite abruptly, however, a small black fox came running right up and sat down directly in their path. Both children were startled by his appearance and cried in unison, "It's him!," but their outcry did not seem to disturb the fox, who sat, still as a stone, his golden eyes fixated upon them.

"You've seen him before, too?" Nicholas whispered to Lark, his eyes never leaving the fox's.

"Yes!" she whispered back, "I only became lost in the forest because I was following him!"

The fox now shook its small head and the children noticed for the first time something around its neck. Without thinking, Nicholas leaned down and reached out to try and remove whatever it was, thinking he had become entangled in something, as Lark cautioned him with a fierce whisper to "be careful!"

The fox did not shy away from Nicholas' advance, instead lifting its head slightly to allow Nicholas better access. With as much delicacy as his mittened hands could muster, Nicholas removed the object from around the fox's neck. As he slowly rose to his feet, he held it out for Lark to see. Her green eyes grew even wider as she saw the most beautiful stone she had ever seen, strung on a dark piece of leather. The stone was no larger than an acorn, but its color was unlike anything the children could have imagined. It seemed to be ALL colors, beautiful greens and blues and golds and reds, all at the same time. The color changed and shifted like mercury as they gazed upon it, giving it the illusion of perpetual motion.

"It's beautiful!" Lark said in an excited whisper, "Why it's the most beautiful thing I've ever seen!"

Nicholas simply nodded silently. Then, an instant later, thrust out his hand to her saying, "You must keep it! It's yours!"

"I couldn't possibly... " she objected quietly, even as her small, bare hand was reaching for it.

But once her hand was close enough to take the stone, the fox begin growling softly. The two froze completely as they looked back to the fox, who they had almost forgotten was there. They exchanged glances as Lark withdrew her hand. Again, she tried reaching for it, more slowly this time, and again the fox emitted a low, guttural noise that sounded somewhat threatening.

"I. .I guess I'm not meant to have it, Nicholas." Lark said sadly.

"I don't understand." he replied, confused. But as he stood there, trying to make sense of the situation, the fox wound itself around his legs, rubbing his head against Nicholas, seeming to approve of him as the keeper of the stone.

"Ok, little fellow," Nicholas said with a small laugh, "I guess you want me to have this. But, why?"

With that, the fox whipped its bushy tail one last time around Nicholas' leg and dashed away, back into the woods.

"Well," said Lark with a grin, "it seems you really ARE magical, good sir." Now it was her turn to make Nicholas laugh as she bowed her head and gave a deep curtsy.

***

A very short distance later, Helmsgard Manor came into view. No matter how many times Nicholas had seen it, he never ceased to marvel at the sight of both its beauty and sheer size.

"Home sweet home!" said Lark as her pace quickened, eager to be back in her familiar surroundings.

"It really is the most beautiful house in the world," Nicholas said to her.

"How wonderful to live in such a place!"

"Tell me about your home, Nicholas. Is it wonderful, too? It must be to have such a wonderful boy living in it!" Again feeling as though she had spoken in a manner much too heartfelt, Lark lowered her eyes and turned her head. Nicholas noticed, took both her hands in his, and said, "You are the kindest girl I have ever met. Thank you."

And he desperately wanted to tell her everything. Again, the urge to confide in this new friend overwhelmed him, and he wished nothing more than to pour out his heart, his troubles, his thoughts... his everything ... to her. But he didn't dare spoil the moment by burdening her with details of his wretched home or his heartless parents. So he simply said, "Next time!" and sincerely hoped there would be one.

"Now let's not waste a moment; I have wanted to see this place my whole life!" And with that the two children, hands clasped, began racing toward the imposing structure.

Helmsgard Manor sat atop a small hill, the elevation making it even more imposing, though it needed no help in that regard. Constructed of rough stone, with a dark shingled roof and numerous leaded glass windows that were glowing golden with the bright morning sun, the place seemed to Nicholas to be more castle than house. Imposing chimneys and turrets and steeply pitched gables and dormers adorned the roofline, and he stopped and silently took in the grandeur of it all.

"Come on, Nicholas, we're almost there!" Lark's words shook him from the spell the house had cast over him, and he smiled at her as they continued.

After traveling along a winding stone path, lined on each side with ancient trees, they at last reached the house. An imposing set of double doors, dark brown wood with gigantic iron hinges and decorations, seemed to Nicholas to be built for giants, they were so massive. Lark stood on her tiptoes to grab one of the large iron doorknockers and banged away with all her might, yelling "I'm home, everyone!" Nicholas was momentarily startled, feeling surely there must be some more dignified way to announce one's arrival to such a grand dwelling. But he didn't have long to worry about her methods, as moments later, the doors slowly began to open from the middle, creaking their time-worn welcome to the children.

In contrast to the dark, groaning doors, the voice that greeted them was bright and cheery, exclaiming, "Good heavens, my darling, where ever have you been?" The face that soon appeared was every bit as inviting and warm as the voice to which it belonged, and looked nearly identical to Lark's, with large green eyes and auburn hair. The only difference was the lines gently etched into her face, reflecting a lifetime of happiness.

"Mother!" Lark cried, as she inserted herself into the opening between the doors, throwing her arms around the woman's plump waist like she would never let go.

"Oh!" her mother cried, reeling backwards from the loving assault that knocked her completely off balance, and nearly off her feet. She began laughing and said, "I should be terribly cross with you, young lady, but it's quite impossible when you're so tightly wrapped around me!" She pried the girl's arms from around her waist and kneeled down to address her. "But I want to know what on earth has kept you so long!"

Nicholas, still standing just outside the open doors, had been watching the entire scene with great amusement, and something close to envy, except he was not capable of true envy. True envy required an element of self-pity, and for a boy who had nothing, who was given nothing, he expected nothing, and therefore never found cause to feel sorry for himself. But there was an inward realization that this sort of affection between a parent and child was foreign to him, and he felt a momentary pang of sadness.

Lark seemed to suddenly remember the guest of honor she had brought home, and rushed back over to the doors, where she grabbed Nicholas by the hand and dragged him over the threshold, yelling "Mother, look!" She thrust Nicholas roughly towards her mother, making both of them laugh at the sheer force her small body was capable of producing. Nicholas smiled at Lark's mother and politely said "It's very nice to meet you; I'm Nicholas," and extended his hand.

Recognizing Lark's mittens on his hands, her mother exclaimed "Why hello, Nicholas, it's very nice to meet you, but you seem to have put on the wrong pair of mittens!" she smiled at him as she shook his small hand.

"Well, you see... " he started, but was interrupted by Lark's excited proclamation of "Mother, Nicholas saved my life! You see, I got myself lost in the woods as I was following the most darling little black fox, but then I got turned around and lost and then Nicholas came and found me and, oh Mother, may he please stay a while?" the words poured out of her at such a fevered pace that her mother struggled to keep up.

She once again stooped down to be eye level with her daughter and said, "Lark! I haven't the vaguest idea what you're talking about, but no matter, of course he may stay. And while we're enjoying our time together, maybe you can tell me that story again, but a bit slower this time." She kissed her daughter's flushed forehead and rose to her feet.

"Now, Nicholas," she said, "My name is Olga, and we are honored to have you as a guest in our home. If you would like, I would be delighted to show you around" her eyes twinkled as she extended her hand to him, which he took with no hesitation.

"Yes, please!" he responded, still disbelieving that he was a guest in this beautiful place. As he looked around at the impossibly high, vaulted ceilings with their massive iron chandeliers, the staircase in front of them with its ornately carved handrails and balusters, the dappled, golden light dancing throughout the place from the hundreds of windows, his heart was even more full than usual, as he soaked it all in.

Olga led him through the countless rooms where he continued to be astonished and enchanted. The library was filled with thousands upon thousands of books, the living areas were luxuriously appointed with velvet chairs and settees, magnificent tapestries hung throughout the hallways, as suits of armors stood guard over all the exquisite things, their knightly presence warding off anyone or anything who might dare intrude upon the serenity of the place. Nicholas was speechless throughout the tour, prompting Lark to ask,"Are you okay, Nicholas? You haven't said a word!"

Worrying that his silence may be mistaken for aloofness or disinterest, he quickly responded, "Oh, yes, I'm better than okay! I've never seen anything like it in my whole life!" His smile was broad as he looked first at Lark, then at Olga. "I can't thank you enough for welcoming me into your home."

"It's my pleasure, young man," Olga said warmly as she placed her hand on Nicholas' shoulder, "now, if I'm not mistaken, that delicious aroma in the air means breakfast is nearly ready, and we should make our way to the dining room at once!"

Nicholas had been so caught up in looking that his other senses had gone temporarily dull, and he only now noticed that the air was perfumed with the wonderful smells of a meal nearing completion. While he desperately wanted to see every room in Helmsgard Manor, he was keenly aware of

the growing ache in his stomach, a pang with which he was all too familiar, as regular meals were not part of his daily life.

As they made their way to the dining room, they encountered an old lady, who, like Lark and Olga, had a sweet, round face, but her hair was white as snow, wrapped in a neat bun on top of her head.

Her green eyes were no less bright than the other two, but hers shined behind a small pair of spectacles that rested on her delicate nose.

"Well, hello!" she said, quite loudly, raising a hand in greeting, "who do we have here?"

"Why, hello, Mama," said Olga with a big smile, "let me introduce you to our new friend, Nicholas!"

"Yes, yes, bring the child to me, but first of all, I would like to know where YOU have been, young lady!" she pointed a small, craggy finger accusingly at Lark. "Why, we thought we were going to have to set the whole village to looking for you!" her voice was intended to sound firm, but it was so crackly and comical that the entire effect was lost on all who heard. Lark ran over to the lady, embracing her with the same exuberance she had her mother, and the lady responded by pretending to be annoyed, exclaiming "Here, here, child, stop that! You're going to wrinkle my fancy new dress and I'm too old to see well enough to sew another!" But her face could not conceal her delight at the little girl's presence and she seemed to drink in the attention from her granddaughter.

"And who is this strapping fellow? Lark, have you run off and gotten yourself married without telling us about it?" the old lady said with a mischievous grin, causing Lark's cheeks to flush and her mother to say, "Oh, mama, really!"

"No, grandma, this is my friend Nicholas! We met just now in the forest, for you see I had gotten myself lost following a darling little black fox and ... ," as she began once again launching into the tale of her woodland adventure, her grandma cut her off abruptly saying, "A black fox! Oh, my, that IS very special, indeed. For you know that all black foxes are magical, of course."

"Mama, really!" Lark's mother responded, with a slight hint of exasperation to her voice, but an amused expression on her face, as she was quite accustomed to her mother's antics.

"Really, grandma?" Lark cried, as Nicholas' eyes grew wide at the news.

"Well, of course, silly girl! How many black foxes have you ever seen? They say there are only a handful of them in the whole world. It's said that they are black because long ago, a very bad man wanted to rule all the kingdoms of all the world. He tried to destroy the entire population of foxes, for they were the one thing he feared, as their cleverness was well-known . One day, this evil man was wreaking havoc in a village, laying waste to everything and everyone in his path, and drew his sword, which was enormous and black as night, to cut down a child who had fallen in his haste to run for safety. But, at the very moment the enormous blade would have struck the boy's neck, a fox appeared from seemingly out of nowhere, leapt and sunk his sharp teeth into the man's arm, causing him to drop the sword, and allowing the boy time to escape. The fiend cried out, grabbed the heroic fox so tightly he snapped the neck of the poor thing, and the fox fell to the ground, lifeless. The scoundrel then decided the fox's head would make a fine trophy from his day's work and swung his blade downward toward its neck. But, the instant the blade touched him, the fox's bushy fur turned from copper to solid black, and he disappeared.

The children both gasped as the old lady's voice dropped to an almost- whisper.

"Oh yes," she said solemnly, "and that fox not only turned black as night, but at that moment he also gained the power of second sight; he could see into the future. The gift was given to him because he was willing to sacrifice his own life to save another and now he would be able to foresee much of the future, good and bad. And from that time on, any fox born with black fur would be just as magical, but they are the rarest of creatures."

Lark and Nicholas had not moved since this tale began, and they still stood, transfixed, as it ended. It was only when Lark's mother smiled and said, "Ok, mama, you've had your fun, but I know the children are hungry, so let's make our way to the dining room," that the spell was broken.

"But it's true, I tell you!" the older lady cried in protest, waving a small hand animatedly in the air for emphasis. Recalling their extraordinary experience just a short time before, the children exchanged quick glances but neither mentioned the details or the mysterious stone to the adults.

Still trying to steer the children back to non-magical things, Olga remarked, "Nicholas, with all this talk of foxes and forests and such, I failed to properly introduce you. This is my mother, Ingrid. As you can tell, she has lived a very interesting life, and she loves nothing more than to tell a good story."

As Olga placed a hand on each child's shoulder, herding them away from her eccentric mother, the children both looked back at Ingrid, who gave them a knowing wink.

Following a breakfast that seemed to Nicholas to be a feast fit for a king, the two children spent the day exploring the house and the grounds, talking, playing make-believe games, and enjoying every moment of their time together. The time seemed to slip away before they even realized it, and soon it was late afternoon.

The elaborate dinner that evening included roast pheasant, venison, parsnips and potatoes, cheeses and dark bread with just a hint of sweetness, and a dessert of gingerbread with spiced pears, all served on a massive table with gigantic candelabras showering light over the dishes and diners. Even better than the succulent food was the presence of Lark's family. Her father, Anders, who had been out looking for his daughter, was tall and strong, with broad shoulders and a square jaw-line. His dark hair was wavy, like Nicholas', and he had a thick, luxurious beard, which he stroked thoughtfully as they conversed over the meal. Nicholas liked him right away, as he was affable and laughed easily. The meal lasted well into the evening, and Nicholas was so mired in his enjoyment of the occasion that he completely lost track of time.

As he happened to glance to one of the previously light-filled windows, he realized with surprise that it was now fully night-time and he knew he must leave at once. Momentarily forgetting his manners, he abruptly stood up and announced, "I'm so sorry, but I must go!"

Lark's parents realized they had not stopped to consider Nicholas' journey home, or the worry his late arrival would cause his parents. Olga immediately stood and walked over to where he was, apologizing profusely for her lapse in judgment.

"I'm so sorry, child, we have kept you much too long. It's just that you are such lovely company, and we've enjoyed having you so much." Her words were warm and sincere and the smile she gave Nicholas was as nourishing as the magnificent meal he had enjoyed.

"Oh, it's quite alright, and I cannot thank you enough for your hospitality," Nicholas replied, "it's just that I really must be going now, it's very late." He did not bother them with the detail that his absence had likely not been noticed by his parents and, if it had, would only be a source of ire and not concern.

The entire family escorted him back to the massive front doors, with Ingrid handing him a linen cloth filled with bread and cheese for the trip home, as if he could possibly eat another bite. He received it gratefully, and thanked them all as heartily as he knew how, declining their kind offer to loan him a horse from their stable for the journey. Parting with his new friend, Lark, was particularly difficult. He couldn't quite explain it, but he felt like he had known this girl for as long as time had existed. As he was stepping out the door into the frigid winter air, she cried, "Wait!" and he immediately froze in place.

She disappeared briefly back into the front parlor and came back with her mittens. She handed them to Nicholas and, anticipating his refusal, said sharply "Shh! I won't hear a word about it. It's frightfully cold and you have no mittens. You will take these and wear them. And one day, perhaps, when it's warm, you can visit again and return them to me." Her eyes lit up and she smiled at him.

Knowing it was futile to refuse, and anxious for any reason to return... to this place, to these people, to this girl...he simply returned her smile and said, "Thank you. Thank you all. For everything."

"Are you sure you'll be alright finding your way home?" Anders asked, as they were saying their goodbyes. "I have a stable full of horses who would love to go for a late-night ride!"

"You're kind to offer," Nicholas replied, "but I could make it home blindfolded, as many times as I've done it!"

"Well, I daresay you could, but maybe just for tonight, you keep your eyes open." Olga said warmly.

"And watch out for the black fox!" Ingrid crowed, recalling the rapt attention Lark and Nicholas had given her tale.

"I will!" Nicholas cried, as he headed back down the pathway.

He felt as though his feet never touched the earth on that frigid walk home, so light were his footsteps. When he returned home, he was unsurprised that his parents were already fast asleep, utterly undisturbed by their son's absence.

***

The next morning they shook him awake roughly, demanding to know why he had returned with no money. He felt so protective of Lark and her wonderful family and the whole magical evening, that he did something he never did. He lied. He told them that he had earned some money at the blacksmith shop, but that the hole in his pants pocket must have led to it falling out on his way home.

"Useless," his mother called him.

"Worthless," his father grumbled at him. "Get out all the earlier today and make up for what you cost us, boy!"

"Yes, father." Nicholas responded with an unerring patience and grace that never ceased to agitate and infuriate his parents. He was given no breakfast, and was directed out into the snowy day once again to find what work he could.

As he was leaving, he heard his mother's shrill voice call after him, demanding, "What are these? Where did you get these?"

He turned around to find her holding the soft red mittens that Lark had given him, and he was immediately angry with himself for not taking care to hide them.

"Mother, those were given to me by a friend in town..."

"Friend?" his mother scoffed, "Who would want to be friends with such a stupid, lazy boy?"

"He must have stolen them," his father growled "I told you he wasn't working when he went into town. He's as deceitful as he is lazy!"

With that, his father snatched the mittens from his mother and tossed them into the small fire that was burning in the kitchen.

"No!" Nicholas cried, even as he realized it was too late to do anything. He could only stand and watch as the beautiful gift from his beautiful friend turned to ash. Utterly defeated, he hung his head and didn't resist when his father grabbed him by the arm and thrust him back towards the door.

"Out!" his father barked at him, "and don't come back until you've decided to work and bring home the money you owe us instead of robbing people blind, you shameful scoundrel!"

Nicholas could hear his mother's gravely laughter as she took in the scene, enjoying Nicholas' humiliation as he tripped and fell when his father released his arm.

Nicholas was crushed by his parents' cruelty. Though he long ago became accustomed to their heartless ways, it was a different matter altogether when it was directed, not at him, but at his friend, who had done nothing but show him kindness and selflessness.

He was walking slowly, gutted by the loss of the gift, and had not gone far from home when he remembered the stone the fox had given him the night before. He reached in his pocket (which, in reality, had no hole) and breathed a sigh of relief to find it still there. He ran his fingers over it, marveling at how impossibly smooth it was. He took it from his pocket and watched the colors change for a moment, then continued on. As he reached the edge of the forest, he was still clasping it tightly in his fist.

From the corner of his eye, he saw a flash of movement just inside the woods, and turned to see what was there. To his astonishment, it was the black fox from the day before, now sitting just within the forest's border.

"Why, hello!" Nicholas called to him, and the fox nodded his small head in acknowledgment. Wondering if the stone in his hand had anything to do with the fox's appearance, Nicholas now held it up for him to see.

"Is this why you're here?" he called to the fox as he made his way closer to where the fox was sitting.

Again, the fox gave a small nod of acknowledgment.

Nicholas paused for a moment to take in the sheer strangeness of the situation, but he was delighted to his very core to find he could apparently summon this new friend. But why? He couldn't figure it out, but felt it must be something connected with his sweet new friend whose gift had been so recently destroyed.

Nicholas was now just beside the fox, and he crouched down slowly and sat on the ground.

"I do wish you could talk, Mr. Fox, so that you could explain to me about this strange stone you've placed in my care. It seems as though you and this stone are connected. And maybe it has something to do with Lark, since she was there when we met."

The fox now placed a small furry paw on Nicholas' leg, and stared intently at him. As Nicholas returned his gaze, still holding the stone, to his complete amazement, the forest all around him began disappearing! As though some force of nature had suddenly descended upon it, uprooting everything in its path, suddenly the trees, the ground, everything except Nicholas and the fox, seemed to be carried off in some sort of swirling vortex.

Dumbfounded, Nicholas watched his woodland surroundings vanishing before his very eyes, but soon realized new surroundings were being created in their place as he watched, and they seemed instantly familiar. He was back at Helmsgard Manor! Nicholas and his furry companion were swallowed up into this new scene and found themselves right back in the place where Nicholas had felt so warm and welcome. He could see and hear and smell everything in the dwelling, but felt weightless and seemed to move without meaning to. It was only for a moment, but he was able to see the entire family gathered around the dining table, eating their breakfast and chatting amiably with one another, bright morning light streaming through the windows. Although his body felt very foreign to him, his heart felt the familiar warmth he had experienced there just the evening before.

Before he even had time to speak or call out, though, the scene vanished and Nicholas found himself back on the ground in the forest, the trees, rocks, ground, and everything else, restored to their previous place. He was speechless, and as he was trying to form some sort of coherent thought, without warning, the black fox dashed off into the forest, leaving Nicholas bewildered and just a little frightened. What did it all mean? He had not the slightest guess, but a feeling deep inside him was growing which told him he must see Lark again. And soon.

For now, however, Nicholas knew he must make his way quickly into the village to seek work before the tradesmen and shop owners started their busy days. He practically ran the rest of the way into the village, energized by his most unexpected morning adventure. He was fortunate to find good work that day, with a kind man by the name of Mr. Krum who was the local blacksmith. Nicholas earned a tidy sum working for him, and took it home to his parents, who he found eating their supper without him, and who had prepared him nothing. However, he did not go to bed hungry, because Mr. Krum had been kind enough to prepare a late afternoon meal for the both of them, for which Nicholas was now grateful a second time.

The next morning, Nicholas was up even earlier than usual. He had decided as he drifted off to sleep the previous night that he would somehow make his way back to Helmsgard Manor the very next day. He rose and dressed soundlessly, in order to not wake his parents, and slipped out the door before the sun was even rising in the winter sky.

It was a brutally cold, dark morning as he made his way towards the forest. He knew that finding his way in those conditions might prove tricky, but he could not bring himself to give up on his plan; the pull of both the place and its occupants was undeniable. And so it was that Nicholas found himself deep in the dark woods that morning, heading in the direction of Helmsgard Manor.

He had traveled quite a ways and knew he must be getting close to the forest's edge where he would see the pathway to the home. But he found himself disoriented, and became rather hopelessly turned around. The darkness of the early morning was amplified by the shade of the towering trees, and his usual keen sense of direction seemed to suffer because of it. Though he was not frightened, he was distressed at the loss of precious time this delay was causing him. He had only a small window of time in which to make his spontaneous visit, and he did not want a moment to be wasted.

As he stood there, trying to acclimate to the darkness, he felt something brush against his leg. Startled, he jumped, then stood perfectly still trying to make out anything he could with the little sight he had. He had not realized it, but out of sheer nervousness, he had began fumbling with the colorful stone (which he now kept with him at all times) in his pocket and he suddenly knew the source of the sensation. It must be the black fox!

He crouched on the ground and whispered, "Is it you?" into the frigid air.

A funny little trilling sound, followed by a furry body nudging his hand told him that it was, indeed, his little friend, and this time he allowed Nicholas to gently stroke his head.

"I'm very happy you're here, sir" Nicholas said cheerfully "you seem to always know just when I need a friend."

Nicholas stood up, and the fox began walking in circles around Nicholas' legs. Confused at first, Nicholas soon realized the fox wanted him to follow his lead, and he did so without hesitation. The soft light of morning was just beginning to break and filter through the trees, and Nicholas was able to see just enough to follow closely behind the fox. Soon, the crowd of trees began thinning, and Nicholas realized they were approaching the path to Helmsgard Manor.

"We did it!" he cried, as he leaned down to his friend, who had navigated the way, "how can I ever thank you?"

The fox paused only momentarily, and Nicholas could have sworn he saw a small wink from one of his eyes. Then, as he had before, the fox disappeared back into the woods.

Nicholas yelled after him, "You are a good friend and I am at your service!" unsure if his words were heard, so quickly the fox ran away.

Turning his attention now to his destination, he began making his way down the winding path that led to the most extraordinary place he had ever known.

As he walked, he began to worry. What if they would not welcome his surprise visit? What if they found it, and him, intrusive and unwanted, just as his own family did? What if they weren't even home and he had come all this way for nothing?

None of these thoughts slowed him, however. Somewhere deep inside, he knew they would be home, and they would welcome him. They just had to.

Finally he reached the massive wooden doors, took a deep breath, and knocked, startling himself as he was reminded of the deep resonation of the massive doorknockers.

The passing moments felt like an eternity, and Nicholas became conscious of the fact that he was holding his breath in anticipation. He would not have to do so for long, however, as the doors soon opened and he saw the familiar face of Lark's mother, Olga, smiling down at him. In that instant, basking in the radiance of her presence, he knew his decision to visit had been the right one.

"Why, Nicholas!" she said, clearly surprised but happy to see him, "What on earth brings you here this morning?"

Turning her head back inside, she called out to her daughter, "Lark, come down here, you have a visitor!" then quickly shuttled Nicholas inside.

"Come in, come in! It's freezing out there!" she seemed to not notice the absence of the mittens Lark had given him, for which Nicholas was thankful. Just as he was removing his thin jacket, he saw Lark descending down the stairs at a full run, stopping just short of the landing to hop on the banister and slide the last few feet to the floor.

"Lark!" her mother cried sharply, "How many times have I told you that is very unladylike and dangerous and..."

Lark seemed not to hear her mother at all as she ran over to where her friend was standing and threw her arms around him, crying, "Nicholas! What a wonderful surprise!"

Nicholas was immediately overcome with the same feeling of cozy familiarity that he had felt when he first met her, and he hugged her back tightly.

Unfortunately for Nicholas, Lark's eye was quick to notice the missing mittens, and she grabbed his hands and asked "Where on earth are the mittens, Nicholas? You didn't lose them, did you? Because if you did, I'll go right upstairs and find you another pair and ..."

"No," he interjected, "I didn't lose them. It's just that..."'

Olga, sensing a growing discomfort from the boy, quickly excused herself, saying she needed to go check on breakfast. Nicholas was relieved by her departure, because he found himself unable to keep the truth from Lark.

Lark, who shared her mother's kind heart and desire to help, led him to the library where he sank into a sumptuous burgundy velvet chair that was so large it threatened to swallow him whole.

"Now," Lark said, as she sat herself across from him in a stately chair of carved wood with a leather seat, "tell me what happened."

With that, Nicholas found himself, to his horror, pouring out his heart to her, sparing no detail about his family, his home, and the struggles of his everyday life.

Her eyes filled with tears as he spoke, but she would not allow herself to cry because she knew it would further add to his embarrassment. She had never imagined anyone lived in such a world as Nicholas, devoid of love or warmth. How remarkable, she thought, that he was so gracious, so kind, since he had never been shown grace or kindness. She silently vowed to do everything she could to try and make up for all the goodness that life had denied him.

"So, anyway," he concluded in a voice that was quiet but not defeated "that's what happened. I'm so very sorry. They were the loveliest mittens, and you were so kind to give them to me." His blue eyes widened as he searched her face for any sign that she may be reluctant to remain friends with someone so poor in both material things and love.

Not knowing what else to do, Lark took his hands, looked into his eyes and said as sincerely as she knew how, "You, Nicholas, are a rare and wonderful boy. I know I can't fix everything for you, but I want you to know I am always right here if you need anything at all. Your parents are fools, and they do not deserve you. One day, I will make it right. I don't know how, but I will."

And he believed her. At that moment, with her hands holding his and her sweet voice drowning out every other thought, he would have believed anything in the world.

The moment was suddenly disrupted by a shrill voice crying, "You again? Child, you might as well become a member of the family if you're going to visit us all the time!" Ingrid's smiling face peeked in through the half- closed doors as she discovered the children.

"Hello, Miss Ingrid!" Nicholas greeted her with a wide grin.

"Hello, Nicholas!" she responded, coming into the room and greeting him with a comically firm handshake, her withered little hand even smaller than his.

"Grandma, Nicholas has surprised us with a visit, isn't that grand?" Lark smiled at her grandmother adoringly.

"It is, indeed!" Ingrid exclaimed, then grabbed each of the children by a hand and began tugging them in the direction of the door claiming, "But enough brooding in this dark, old room, I smell breakfast and you growing boys and girls need to eat!"

Nicholas and Lark looked at one another and laughed, as the tiny woman dragged them out of the library and into the hallway.

After a delicious breakfast, Nicholas knew he had better be on his way. As before, the entire family escorted him to the door as he was leaving. And, as before, Nicholas felt a desperate urge to stay. But he ventured out into the bright cold morning, determined to do what was expected of him.

As he approached the woods, he saw a movement in the brush, and he immediately knew his friend, the fox, had come once again to walk with him. Having anticipated this, Nicholas had asked if he might bring some scraps from the breakfast table to feed him, and Lark's family had willingly obliged. Ingrid had even joked with him about it being a "fine idea to keep those magical creatures on your good side."

Sure enough, as Nicholas began making his way back into the woods, the little black fox appeared at his feet, seemingly out of nowhere. Nicholas realized he had, again, unconsciously pulled the stone from his pocket and was holding it.

"Hello, my good fellow!" Nicholas greeted him, "Since you've been most helpful and kind to me, I brought you a little something. I enjoyed the most wonderful breakfast with our friend, Lark, and have brought you a sampling of some most delicious treats!" He kneeled down and unfolded the cloth, revealing sweets and savories of the most delectable sort. The fox nudged Nicholas' hand in gratitude, and proceeded to devour the breakfast. When he was finished, he and Nicholas made their way back through the forest, parting at the tree line that marked the border of woods.

"Goodbye, my friend, I hope to see you again soon!" Nicholas reached down and patted the fox on the head and the fox darted back into the thicket.

Nicholas was happy to once again find good work that day in the village, this time with Mrs. Berg, who was the village baker. He enjoyed his work there more than any other place, and Mrs. Berg was a wonderful employer who patiently taught him how to bake all sorts of mouth-watering treats. She also insisted he "sample" everything they made, telling him he must never sell anything he himself had not tried. She had convinced Nicholas this step was simply about being a good steward of your creations, but in reality she, like all the other villagers, knew about Nicholas' parents and home and his need.

After a very busy day, Nicholas was walking back home, with a full belly and a full heart, having enjoyed his day more than almost any day he could remember. He decided to again take the longer way home through the woods, since he had time and he hoped to see the little fox, of whom he had grown quite fond. He had even thought of a name for his friend, since it seemed to Nicholas that anyone so kind and helpful should have a name. He would call him Finn, and he hoped the name was suitable to his friend. Having realized the beautiful stone the fox had given him seemed to have the power to summon him, he removed it from his pocket, rubbing it gently, and looked around anxiously to see if it worked.

He was not disappointed, as very soon the fox revealed himself, appearing from behind a bush and waiting for Nicholas to walk over. When Nicholas reached the fox, he sat down beside him, and this time the fox curled up in his lap. Nicholas was completely delighted by this development, and gently petted his soft fur. While they sat there, Nicholas said, "I've been thinking about something for a while, and that something is that you should have a name. Would it be alright if I called you Finn?" In response, the fox nudged Nicholas' hand with his head and seemed to almost purr.

Abruptly, however, the fox stood up, faced Nicholas, and began staring intently into his eyes, as he had before. Nicholas had no choice but to return his gaze, still holding the stone, which he now felt pulsing in his hand. As before, as soon as their eyes locked, their surroundings began disappearing in a whirl, seemingly carried off on the very wind itself. And again, as everything around him was disappearing, the interior of Helmsgard Manor was taking its place. In just a matter of moments, Nicholas and Finn found themselves again in the grand home, again strangely able to employ all of their senses, but unable to dictate their movements.

This time, however, the scene before them was quite different. They were in the enormous library, where the shelves of books lined the walls and reached all the way to the impossibly-high ceilings. Lying on one of the large tufted sofas, nearly lost in the size of the thing, was Lark, and she was crying softly.

Unable to speak, all Nicholas could do was watch, helplessly, as Lark's mother, then father, then grandmother, came in to try and console her. Though he could only pick up parts of their quiet conversation, Nicholas clearly heard Lark say, "I can't believe he's gone; I barely got to know him, and he was so kind..." before burying herself in her mother's arms, sobbing.

Nicholas was panicked by her words, wondering who she could be talking about, but fearing, though he didn't wish to acknowledge it, that she must be talking about him. After all, who else could it be? She had told him on their walk in the forest the day they met, that, though her life was happy and full, she had no friends or company beyond her immediate family. But what did she mean when she said "gone?" He didn't want to think on it too deeply, as it gave him a growing sense of dread.

Just as this realization began to take hold of Nicholas, however, the scene once again changed, and he found himself back at the forest's edge, with Finn standing beside him. He was shaken, and sat down, hoping Finn would comfort him, but the little fox scurried away back into the woods before Nicholas could stop him. Feeling more confused and frightened than he ever had in his life, Nicholas sat for a very long time. He couldn't help remembering what Ingrid had told them about the power of black foxes to see the future. He felt surely Finn had shared this vision with him for a reason, but why? Was he warning him about something he could prevent, or simply showing him an inevitable fate?

When he could ponder no longer and the sky began to darken, Nicholas knew he must continue his walk home, but decided he would not go through the forest after all. Suddenly it seemed to be more unsettling and uncertain than it had been just a few moments before.

Nicholas' sleep was tormented that night as he agonized over Lark's possible prophesy. Visions of terrible fates flashed through his mind as sleep eluded him until the earliest hours of the morning, when he finally fell into a fitful sleep. He woke up much later than he should have, to the ire of his parents who ridiculed and berated him as he tried to hastily make his way out for the day.

Over the following weeks, Nicholas continued to secretly visit Lark and her family, and came to feel as though he were a member in his own right.

They were endlessly kind and generous to him, but in a way that never felt like pity. They seemed to truly enjoy his company, and each visit was more merry and comfortable than the last. And as for Lark, the two of them became inseparable. Their love was the purest love, which only the purest souls, like those that belong to children, may possess. They came to share a bond that enabled each of them to know the unspoken thoughts and feelings of the other.

Finn remained Nicholas' faithful companion, meeting him each morning at the forest's edge and accompanying him to and from the village if he traveled through the woods that day. Lark came to love the little fox too, as they all spent time together on woodland walks. When Nicholas told Lark about how the stone and the fox's powers combined to allow him to see Helmsgard Manor, her family, and, perhaps, the future, she was not at all alarmed as he feared she would be. She was delighted, and encouraged Nicholas to continue to use this magical power whenever possible. Even when he confided in her about the upsetting scene he had witnessed during one such event, she showed no fear or hesitance in her encouragement.

"Nicholas," she said, taking both his hands in hers, "I used to be afraid of things. Lots of things. Since I met you, somehow nothing seems frightening to me anymore. It's as though I know things will always turn out okay, even if I don't understand how." Hearing this, and before he could stop himself, Nicholas leaned over and gave her a small kiss on the cheek. Lark laughed, then returned the kiss, Nicholas' plump cheeks reddening slightly as she did.

The day Nicholas revealed the secret to her was a happy one, and he and Finn had traveled back to Nicholas' home with their steps light and their hearts merry.

In the very early hours of the very next morning, he had just fallen into a deep, dreamless sleep when the air was pierced with a noise that caused him to sit upright in bed, immediately certain that the noise was related to his vision of Lark in distress over a grave loss.

Without thinking, he flung off his thin blanket and ran to the front door of his tiny, forlorn home and what he saw filled him with an anguish he had not known was possible.

There, just beyond his front door was Finn, lying motionless, an arrow piercing his small body. A few yards away, Nicholas saw his father, his bow in hand, his face twisted into a wicked smile.

Nicholas' cry of anguished disbelief resonated through the frost-heavy morning air as he ran over to his friend, desperate to see if there was yet life left in his small body. Falling to the ground, he collapsed in tears as he realized the arrow had hit its mark with precision, fatally piercing Finn's body. Nicholas's father watched gleefully as his son cradled the fallen fox in his arms, softly whispering words he could not make out. He walked over, and hissed "You think I don't know how you've been spending your time, you stupid boy? I've been following you, and I know all about your little adventures." Nicholas looked up at him, his tear-stained face eliciting no sympathy from the cruel man.

"That's right, you simpleton. I know all about the girl, and your visits to her house. Ashamed of your family, are you? Our home isn't good enough for you now, is that it? You would rather spend time with strangers and vermin like this dead creature than your family. Then so be it. Leave, and never darken my doorway again." His father spat on the ground beside Nicholas and Finn, and walked back into the house.

Hours passed, and still Nicholas sat, holding Finn as his warm body grew cold in Nicholas' arms. Not knowing what else to do or where to go, he walked into the forest, still cradling Finn, heading to Helmsgard Manor.

The journey took much longer than usual, as Nicholas' steps were slow and plodding. He was so grief-stricken, he failed to realize when he arrived at the path to the home. He hesitated only a moment; he wanted nothing more than to shield Lark from any hurt or pain, but he felt an obligation to let her know about their friend.

When he reached the massive doors, he cradled Finn in one small arm, and used the other hand to grasp the heavy door knocker and announce his arrival. It was Ingrid's face who greeted him when the doors opened, and she immediately noticed his despairing, tear-stained face, and the beautiful but lifeless black fox at his feet.

"Oh, you poor dear, what on earth... ?" she didn't hesitate to bend down and touch the fox's cold little body before wrapping her arm around Nicholas and shuffling him into the house.

"But Finn," he managed to say, with a quavering voice, "I can't just leave him... "

"Of course not, darling." Ingrid said softly, "I will bring him in just as soon as I get you out of the cold." True to her word, once Nicholas was safely ensconced in the warmth of the enormous foyer, Ingrid disappeared momentarily, returning with a soft, pale blue blanket. Stepping back out into the bitter cold air of the morning, she lovingly wrapped Finn in the blanket and brought him inside. Nicholas followed her into the drawing room, where Ingrid placed the fox on a large ottoman and stroked the fur on his unresponsive head. Nicholas watched, with the smallest hope that his friend could be revived. Ingrid sang softly to him, a song which Nicholas did not recognize, and whose words were of an ancient language he did not know. But the fox remained still, and Nicholas' hope dwindled.

By this time, Lark had heard the commotion, and was running down the enormous staircase at full speed. "Nicholas!" she cried, as she spotted him in the drawing room, unaware of the circumstances, and happy, as always, to see her friend, "What a wonderful sur-" she stopped mid-sentence as she saw first Nicholas' face, then her grandmother with the lifeless fox.

She immediately ran over and grabbed Nicholas, crying, "What happened, Nicholas? What's the matter with Finn?" her own tears now filling her green eyes.

"He ... he's dead!" saying the words brought a fresh wave of anguish to Nicholas and he collapsed in Lark's waiting arms. She, too, began crying and looked at Ingrid with eyes full of desperation.

In that moment, Lark collapsed onto a small sofa, sobbing, and Nicholas immediately realized the scene before him was the one he had glimpsed that day when he and Finn were in the forest. He had never guessed Lark's despair would have been caused by their friend being harmed so cruelly.

"Grandma, can you help him? There has to be a way ..."

Ingrid looked sadly at her granddaughter and Nicholas, slowly shaking her head, and said "I'm sorry, child, I can do nothing for him."

By this time, Lark's parents had both come into the room, full of questions about all the noise they had heard. Taking in the entire scene in a quick glance, they both immediately realized what had happened. Olga rushed to her daughter's side while Anders walked over to where the little swaddled fox lay on the ottoman.

Putting a gentle hand on Nicholas' shoulder he asked quietly, "What happened, Nicholas?" and Nicholas, who did not have the strength to hold anything back at that point, told Anders the whole story. Anders' jaw visibly clenched as he heard of the cruelty of Nicholas' father, marveling that anyone could behave so callously towards their own child. He did not show his anger to the children, though, knowing that, at that moment, what they needed was compassion and comfort.

Anders took the bundle of fox and blanket into his arms gently and said, "We will find a place for him to be at rest. The forest, I think. .."

Lark replied, "Yes, he would want that," while Nicholas could only nod sadly in agreement.

Anders left the room with Finn, returning a short time later with a small mahogany box. It was a beautiful piece with intricate carvings and the children felt it would be a fitting final resting place for their noble and handsome friend. Anders had lovingly placed the little fox inside, leaving the soft blue blanket tucked around him.

After hastily pulling on their overcoats and hats, the group made their way outside, and began walking towards the forest. The howling wind seemed to echo their sadness, and not a word was spoken between them.

Eventually, they came to a lovely spot, not too far into the woods, where a little icy stream cut a path through a small clearing. It was a beautiful, tranquil spot, and they all knew it was the perfect place for Finn. Anders gently placed the box just under a large, thorny bush, hoping the brambles would be a deterrent for any curious woodland animals. They all stood silently for a moment, listening to the quiet rush of the water and the crackling of icy branches overhead as they shifted in the wind.

41

At last Anders said, "Would anyone like to offer any words?" and Nicholas quietly replied, "I would."

"Finn was my friend, and I will miss him terribly. He never hurt anyone and he didn't deserve this. He was funny, and smart, and kind, and always knew when I needed him. And he gave me the best gift I've ever gotten." He looked at Lark with a smile, "I don't know how or why he led me to her... to all of you . . .but I will be forever grateful that he did. Goodbye, Finn. I am sorry I couldn't be there for you like you were for me."

As no one could think of anything further or more fitting to say, they all stood soundlessly, Lark and Nicholas squeezing each other's hand, and the rest simply offering a eulogy of silence.

Eventually, the adults decided it was time to take the children back to Helmsgard Manor, as the weather was worsening and a heavy snowfall was beginning to creep in.

"May we stay just a little longer, Mother?" Lark asked when Olga quietly mentioned leaving.

Olga looked at Anders who nodded and then answered her daughter's question with a small kiss on her head and a whispered, "Of course," then she, Anders, and Ingrid began slowly walking back towards home.

The children settled themselves on the freezing ground by Finn's little box, and sat silently for a very long time. When Nicholas finally spoke, it was in a quiet voice, asking, "Lark, do... do you think Finn brought us together for a reason? I know it sounds crazy, but I can't help thinking that he showed up at just the right time in just the right place for us to meet. It has to mean something."

Lark smiled at her friend. "I don't think it sounds crazy at all, Nicholas. I think you're exactly right. There's no other explanation. I just don't know what we're supposed to do now that he...," her voice trailed off as she tried to will herself not to cry.

Nicholas put his arm around her and she lay her head on his shoulder. He had no answers, and all he could offer her was his presence.

Suddenly, Nicholas remembered something. Reaching into his pocket, he told Lark, "Close your eyes," which she did without hesitation, trusting him implicitly.

Taking her hand, which was bare and cold since she had not stopped to find her mittens before leaving home, he placed the stone in it, curling her fingers around it to keep her from dropping it, then placing his hand over hers.

"Oh!" she cried as she felt the cold, weighty stone. As she opened her hand, she and Nicholas both grew wide-eyed as they realized it was pulsing rapidly, the colors changing wildly like some energized kaleidoscope.

Without warning, the stone shot high into the air, raining down droplets of color and light and hovering in place just out of the children's grasp.

Nicholas and Lark both jumped to their feet and looked at one another, startled, their mouths agape. They would not have long to take in the scene that was happening above them, however, as what was happening around them suddenly became just as extraordinary.

Every creature of the forest was emerging and approaching them. Raccoons, squirrels, birds of every color plumage, all the animals that inhabited the forest seemed to be drawn to where Lark and Nicholas were standing. They made no hesitation as they drew near, all of them, hundreds of them, filling the area all around the two friends. Lark was frightened by all of this and clung tightly to Nicholas, who was too mesmerized by it all to be afraid.

The animals continued streaming in from the trees and thickets... wolves, deer, owls, and every imaginable creature seemed to materialize out of nowhere to join the scene. Once the forest seemed to have emptied itself of all living things, Lark finally lifted her face, which she had buried in Nicholas' shoulder, and took it all in. The animals were all still and silent, with lowered heads and closed eyes. It seemed to the children as though they were showing their reverence for one of their own, and the children were soon enchanted by their display.

The stone remained over the area, but now concentrated its eruption of color, and light, and magic over the brambly bush under which Finn had been placed. It seemed to the children as though the small stone must contain a thousand magnificent stained glass windows, which it now poured in rainbow shards over the little mahogany box, the colors mixing with the pure whiteness of the falling snow.

Without warning, the ground shuddered below their feet, and the lid of the box began trembling. A booming thunderclap sounded and suddenly the lid was flung forcefully from its position, and the stone fell to the ground, the cascading of color and light abruptly ceasing as it did. The silence in the moment was the most complete silence the children had ever experienced. Lark and Nicholas dared not breathe as their eyes fixed upon the box. The multitude of animals surrounding them now lifted their heads and began stamping their feet, snorting, braying, the chipmunks chittering and birds squawking a melody of anticipation.

Suddenly, there was a movement from within the box, the blanket shifting and billowing, and to the children's astonishment, the tiny black head of their beloved Finn appeared, his eyes radiating a brightness they would have never thought possible. It was as though his eyes had BECOME the color, the light, the magic. They shone, mesmerizing all the creatures who were gathered around, until Finn fully emerged from the box, his tiny feet seeming to levitate briefly before touching solid ground. Then, in an instant, his eyes again became the small onyx orbs they had always been, and he gave his head a brief shake. The stone, which had fallen on the ground just beside him, once again pulsed with the magic which it seemed to have temporarily bestowed upon Finn.

44

"Finn!" the children cried in unison, as the animals continued their noisy celebration.

Finn fixed his eyes upon them, and spoke.

"My friends," he said, in a voice that was at once soft and commanding, and as warm as any fireside chair at Helmsgard Manor.

Lark and Nicholas both gasped in shock to hear him speak, but neither offered any interruption.

"Thank you all for being here. My forest companions, your presence and support will not be forgotten. You may all return to your homes now. I believe my human friends may have some questions for me."

With those words, the other animals turned and began streaming soundlessly back out into the woods until none were left.

"And now, my faithful friends, here we are. I'm certain all of this has left you confused and perhaps even frightened. But you needn't fear, for I am neither specter nor spirit, but simply your friend Finn, as you have always known him. And I am eternally grateful for your loyalty and compassion. I'm sorry for any grief or pain I may have caused either of you, but I had to be sure."

"Be sure of what?" Nicholas asked, his mind still reeling from what was happening.

"That you, both of you, were truly worthy."

"Worthy of what?" Lark asked, more confused than she had ever been.

"Worthy of the gift." Seeing the confusion on their faces increase, Finn continued "Let me explain."

"You have, perhaps, heard the legend that black foxes possess a form of magic." Lark and Nicholas both exchanged knowing glances, remembering the story Ingrid had shared with them, and they nodded in acknowledgment.

"Well, as you can see, the story is true. But you may not know the whole story. Each black fox has the gift of second sight, the ability to see into the future. Not everything, and not all the time. It is a selective gift, and we have very little control over it. But, every black fox has the ability to change one future outcome; one thing they have foreseen which they feel the most strongly about. We cannot interrupt the natural order of the universe by intervening all the time; some of the visions we see we simply have to live with."

"But... " Nicholas interjected, "what does that have to do with us?"

"Ah," Finn replied, "it has everything to do with you, Nicholas. And you, Lark. For you see, you are my chosen story, the one I have decided to protect. The story you are creating, through your care for one another, for me, and for every living thing, is a story of love and selflessness that is bigger than the whole world.

It must never be set off-course, never stray from its intended path, for if it is allowed to flourish without interruption, it will be a light in the darkness for generations to come. Every story in the Universe is precarious, and any little thing can derail or alter it. From this day forward, however, your story will continue undisturbed, and you, too, will be given the gift of vision and immortality, with which you will do wondrous things." His black eyes shone as he spoke, and the children knelt down to be closer to him, disbelieving what they were hearing, yet somehow knowing it was all true.

"But," Lark said in a quiet voice, "what if we aren't worthy? What if we make a mistake? Then your gift, our gift, will have been wasted. Oh, Finn, I could never stand to disappoint you!"

47

Finn smiled a small smile and replied,"Ah but you see, sweet Lark, your question assures me that I made the right decision. Your concern, as always, is for others rather than yourself. You can be certain that any mistakes you make, and you will make them, will all be part of the story as it is meant to be. The gift does not make you perfect, it simply allows you to use your imperfections to bring humanity to your story. The two of you have many years to nurture your path, and both the good and bad you experience along the way will be necessary to help you better understand those you will help."

Lark beamed, and Finn said, "Nicholas, the stone... will you pick it up, please?"

Nicholas did as Finn asked, and held it in his outstretched hand to the waiting fox.

"Not for me" Finn said, "It has always been yours, meant only for the two of you. Now, if you'll indulge me, Nicholas, take Lark's hand with your own, the one holding the stone."

Again, Nicholas did as instructed, and as soon as the two children's hands met, together, with the stone, they both had a vision of children, all over the world, whose dreams and wishes and needs they could actually see!

Startled, Lark pulled her hand away, and the vision ceased.

"You see," Finn said, "you each have a special place in your hearts for children such as yourselves. Nicholas, you have become aware of your gift of being able to help children in distress, though I doubt you know the strength behind it. And Lark, you showed your selflessness towards Nicholas, whose heart is as pure as your own. From now on, the goodness that you both possess will grow and together you will change the world. I know it may sound daunting, perhaps even frightening, but in time it will seem entirely natural to you. This is your destiny."

Lark and Nicholas looked at one another, each wondering if the other felt the same incredible anticipation.

"But what about you, Finn?" Nicholas asked, suddenly concerned for his friend. "What will become of you?"

"As always, your caring nature shines through." Finn smiled at the children.

"When a black fox has chosen the story they wish to preserve, they retire to a hidden realm, high in the snowy mountains, where we live with others of our kind."

"So we will never see you again?" Lark asked, distressed at the thought. "Oh but my dear, that's not so!" Finn replied reassuringly.

In response to the children's questioning looks, Finn said, "Nicholas, the stone you have there. Do you remember when we had only first met and I had to be a bit, well rude, to ensure that it was you who had possession of it?"

Nicholas and Lark both smiled as they remembered Finn's gentle growl.

"I do, indeed. You were quite fierce." Nicholas winked playfully at his little friend.

Finn laughed and said, "I was, wasn't I?" knowing he hadn't been anything of the sort.

"Well, Nicholas, I gave that to you, because it has powers, as you know. Sometimes it gives second sight, sometimes it can alert you to danger, sometimes it just helps you stay connected to someone you care about." He watched in amusement as Nicholas temporarily seemed to forget him and, instead, smiled at Lark.

"Yes, that includes Lark, too. Anytime you want to know she is okay, you just hold the stone and think of her. When the colors pulse and change and swirl, you will know she is well. If ever the stone goes dark, however, you must rush to her immediately. Do you understand?" Nicholas nodded solemnly.

Finn continued, "Lark, you have the blessing of a wonderful family. That, in itself, is magical. They will continue to nurture your giving spirit, and they will be a wonderful example for young Nicholas here, who is not so fortunate. But what you may not realize is your power is as strong as Nicholas' or as the stone. Your heart will make you attuned to children the world over, and one day, you will know why."

"And Nicholas," he continued, "you may find the stone helpful in bringing joy to your own parents, though I know it seems impossible. Every soul can be saved, every life is capable of redemption. Return home. Be patient. Continue to be kind. Through you, they will be changed, and will see that they, too, are part of the magic." Nicholas nodded, and the three stood in silence for a moment.

"It is time for me to go now," Finn said, looking up at the snow continuing to fall, "and for each of you to return home. Be diligent in your care for the stone, and for one another. You are young now, but with each passing day you will find your magic, your gifts, and your love for one another stronger, and you will learn to harness those things to create miracles. I cannot tell you all of your story, for you must find out on your own, but I can tell you that you will love and be loved in ways you never knew possible."

With that, Finn leaped onto a large boulder by the icy stream and the children stood by him. They each took a moment to say their goodbyes, Nicholas shaking his tiny paw and thanking him quietly, Lark scooping him up fully and kissing him, holding like she may never let him go.

When she did, placing him gently upon the boulder once more, Finn closed his eyes and said, "Goodbye, my friends. Until we meet again."

With those words, Finn leaped in the direction of the freezing water, causing the children to gasp. Just before his body reached the brook, however, an impossibly strong, snowy gust of wind blew in, lifted

him skyward in a spiraling cyclone of snow and ice and light, and their friend vanished into the swirling white blizzard.

Lark and Nicholas watched in wonder, neither noticing the frigid air enveloping them nor the snow now falling steadily on and around them.

"He's gone." Lark finally said quietly. "But not for good." Nicholas smiled at her.

"I know." she replied, smiling back. And she did. She knew that whatever may come to pass, she and Nicholas and Finn would always be joined by a magical bond that could never be broken.

You probably know the rest of the story, how the two children, selfless and pure of heart, became the beloved givers of joy over all the world and all the centuries. So now, when you search the skies on Christmas Eve for the faintest glimpse of a sleigh or magical reindeer, don't forget to watch for a flash of black on the ground, off in the distance. For it is said that each Christmas Eve, Finn follows their magical journey from below to see his beloved friends fulfilling the story which his gift helped to write.

Made in the USA
Las Vegas, NV
08 November 2021